Angel
AND THE
Box of Time

MICHAEL FOREMAN

RED FOX

A Red Fox Book Published by Random House Children's Books 20 Vauxhall Bridge Road, London SW1V 2SA
A division of The Random House Group Ltd London, Melbourne, Sydney, Auckland, Johannesburg and agencies throughout the world.
Copyright © Michael Foreman 1997 1 3 5 7 9 10 8 6 4 2 First published in Great Britain by Andersen Press Ltd 1997 Red Fox edition 2000
All rights reserved. Printed and bound in Hong Kong THE RANDOM HOUSE GROUP Limited Reg. No. 954009
www.randomhouse.co.uk ISBN 0 09 940276 9

Angel was excited. For the first time, she was going to travel with her grandad and see his travelling show. It was very small. All he had was an old truck and a very old wooden box, covered in names.

After driving all day they arrived at a big city. Grandad took strings of coloured lights from the box and decorated his truck. Then he played his pipes until a small crowd gathered. Suddenly the lid of the box flew open and a goat jumped out and danced to the music of the pipes.

Grandad played slowly at first but as the music got faster and faster the goat leapt onto the roof of the truck and danced round and round without missing a single beat of his drumming hooves. He was clearly enjoying himself.

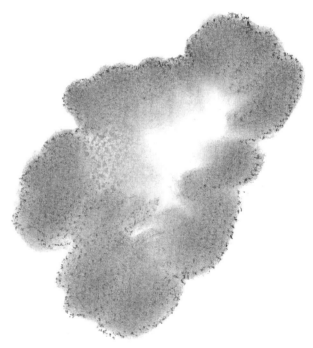

Then there was a BANG! and a big puff of smoke. Before the smoke had cleared, the lights, the pipes and goat had disappeared into the box and the box, Angel and Grandad were in the truck and driving away. They could still hear the crowd cheering.

They stopped soon afterwards at a petrol station. While Grandad was getting petrol and something for them to eat, Angel worried about the goat. He must be hungry. If only she could give him a handful of grass. She looked from the truck at the world of concrete and neon around her. She peeped into one of the tiny airholes in the box and saw . . .

. . . grass. Miles and miles of tall grass, stretching away to a distant horizon and waving in the wind.

Angel felt the wind on her face and felt herself running through the grass. She ran up and over a hill.

There before her was a small town and a small crowd. In the middle of the crowd was an old man who looked like Grandad but couldn't be. It must be Grandad's grandad, she thought. He was playing pipes while a goat danced in the back of an old pick-up truck decorated with flags, without missing a single beat of his drumming hooves.

Suddenly there was a bang
and a puff of smoke and flags,
pipes and goat all disappeared
into an old box.

The crowd cheered and
Angel ran to the box and the
old man smiled as she peeped
in the airhole and saw . . .

. . . snow. Miles and miles of deep snow. Angel felt the chill on her face and felt herself stumbling through the white world towards a cluster of dark wooden shacks and a crowd of people.

And there in the centre of the crowd was a man who looked like Grandad but couldn't be. It must be Grandad's great great-grandad she thought. He was playing pipes while a goat danced along the roofs of the shacks, scattering snow in all directions, without missing a single beat of his drumming hooves.

BANG! The goat and the pipes disappeared into a box in a puff of smoke.

The crowd cheered and Angel came slipping and sliding and peeped into a hole in the box and saw . . .

. . . a river and great cliffs and a canoe pulled up onto a bank. There were tall teepees and camp fires and an excited crowd around a man who looked like Grandad but couldn't be. . . He was playing pipes while a goat danced on a box, without missing a single beat of his drumming hooves.

BANG! Before the puff of smoke cleared, Angel was already at the box and peering into the hole. She saw . . .

. . . an ocean. A wide rolling ocean and plunging up and down on the dark terrifying waves was a ship in full sail.

On the deck of the ship, in a crowd of people, was a man playing pipes. He was an old man who looked like Grandad but couldn't be . . .

A goat danced on a box and drummed out the rhythm with his hooves without missing a single beat until BANG! he disappeared in a puff of smoke.

Angel skidded across the pitching deck and peered into the box and saw . . .

. . . a herd of goats on a stony hillside and in the middle of the goats was an old man, who looked like Grandad but couldn't be, playing pipes.

The man was dancing and as the man danced the goats began turning round and round. They couldn't dance well but they were learning.

Beside the man was a newly-made box. The man smiled as Angel approached.

"Did you make the box?" she asked.

The man nodded. "I've just carved my name."

"What's it for?"

"Ah, Angel," said the old man, "one day it will be yours and then you'll know. Perhaps you will carve your name too."

Angel peeped through one of the tiny holes in the box and saw . . .

. . . nothing. It was dark and empty.

The old man touched his ear. Angel put her ear to the little hole and heard the sound of the ocean, the roaring river, the wind blowing through grass and faint and far away the sounds of a great city. The sounds of her past and her future.

Then she felt a hand on her shoulder.

It was Grandad.

"Wake up, love. It's supper time," he said.

And they drove out of the city and into the future.